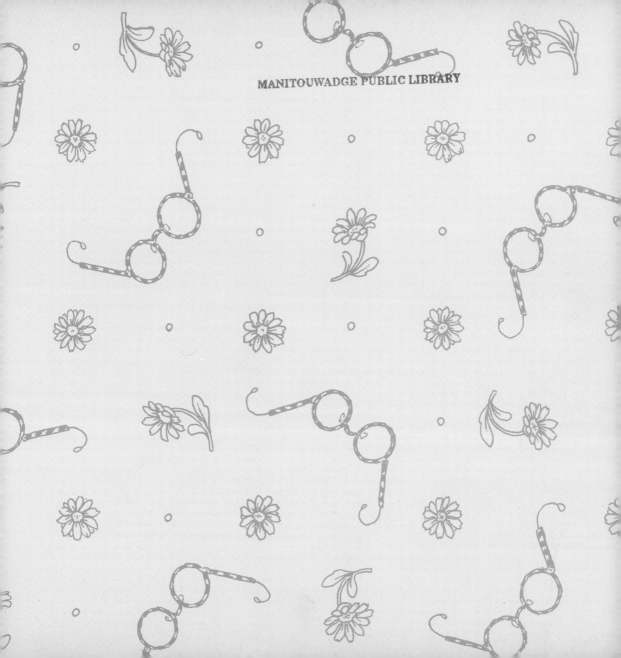

Daisy & Jack

AND THE SURPRISE PIE

For Oliver

Daisy & Jack

and

THE SURPRISE PIE

Prue Theobalds

Uplands Books

One day Jack decided to
make Daisy a surprise pie.

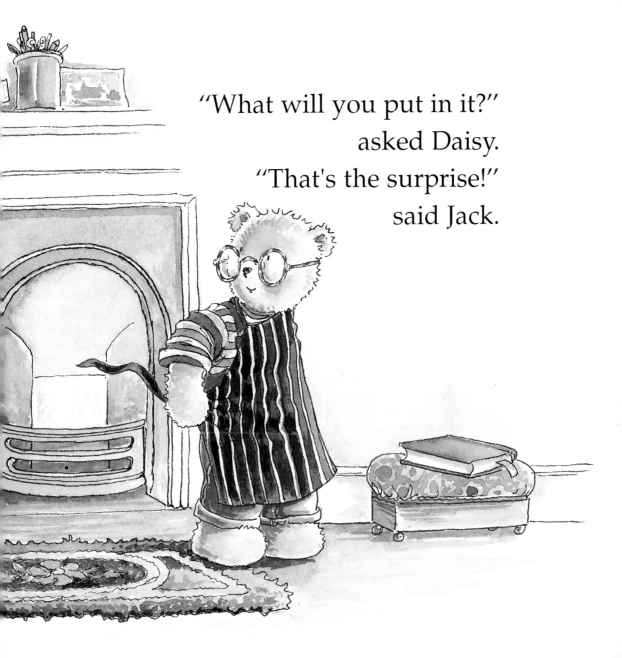

"What will you put in it?"
asked Daisy.
"That's the surprise!"
said Jack.

Jack told Daisy to stay in the garden.

Then he got everything ready.

First he made the pastry in a
big bowl. "Now what shall I
put inside?" he wondered.

He looked in the larder.

There was honey - Daisy liked that -
and chocolate biscuits, apples, raisins,
cherries and nuts.

He mixed them together and put them
in a pie dish.

Then he rolled out the
pastry and covered the
delicious filling.

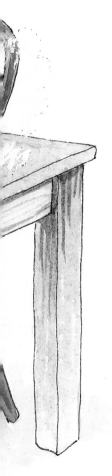

Next he cut a big D out of the left-over pastry, stuck it on top and put the pie in the oven.

"When will my surprise pie be ready?"
called Daisy. "I'm very hungry."

"You will have to wait and see,"
replied Jack.

At last the pie was
cooked. Jack took it
out of the oven and
put it on the window-sill
to cool.

The pie smelt very good!
Daisy carefully lifted the pastry
and peeped inside. "Mmm -
I must have a taste,"
she thought.

It was DELICIOUS.

She decided to have
a little bit more -
and a tiny bit more.

Suddenly she heard Jack
coming back. Quickly
she put the pastry back
and hid.

"Daisy come and try your surprise pie!"
called Jack as he put it on the table.

Daisy sat down and Jack
cut the pie open.

But it was he who had the surprise!

First Published 1997 by Uplands Books
1 The Uplands, Maze Hill, St Leonards-on-Sea,
East Sussex, TN38 0HL, England

ISBN 1 897951 16 7

Printed in Singapore

British Library
Cataloguing-in-Publication Data
A catalogue record for this book is available
from the British Library